**FO**
**M**
**FO**

# FOLLOWING MEOWTH'S FOOTPRINTS

## UNOFFICIAL ADVENTURES FOR POKÉMON GO PLAYERS

### Book Two

## ALex PoLan

Sky Pony Press
New York

First Edition

This is a work of fiction. Names, characters, places, and incidents are from the author's imagination, and used fictitiously.

Sky Pony Press books may be purchased in bulk at special discounts for sales promotion, corporate gifts, fund-raising, or educational purposes. Special editions can also be created to specifications. For details, contact the Special Sales Department, Sky Pony Press, 307 West 36th Street, 11th Floor, New York, NY 10018 or info@skyhorsepublishing.com.

Sky Pony® is a registered trademark of Skyhorse Publishing, Inc.®, a Delaware corporation.

Visit our website at www.skyponypress.com.

Books, authors, and more at SkyPonyPressBlog.com.

10 9 8 7 6 5 4 3 2 1

Library of Congress Cataloging-in-Publication Data is available on file.

Special thanks to Erin L. Falligant.

Cover illustration by Jarrett Williams
Cover colors by Jeremy Lawson
Cover design by Brian Peterson

Print ISBN: 978-1-5107-2158-6
Ebook ISBN: 978-1-5107-2162-3

Printed in Canada

# CHAPTER 1

"The petals are falling!" Devin held up her phone so that Ethan could see her Pokémon GO map.

Sure enough, Dottie's Doughnuts, their favorite Team Mystic gym, was being showered by pink petals from the PokéStop out front.

"Carlo must have set his lure," said Ethan, scanning the sidewalk for his friend.

Carlo was the Gym Leader, and he had decided that every Saturday morning, he would set a lure to bring more customers into Dottie's shop. That's how Team Mystic took care of their favorite gym— and made sure it stayed open!

Any moment now, Pokémon GO players would show up to see which wild Pokémon the lure was attracting. *And hopefully they'll buy lots of doughnuts, too*, thought Ethan.

He took a bite of Dottie's famous Jigglypuff doughnut, which was frosted pink, with candy eyes and chocolate-kiss ears.

She'd been making them for a few weeks now, along with a couple of other Pokémon specials. Her Butterfree doughnut was gluten- and dairy-free. And then there was Dad's personal favorite: the Drowzee, which was served with a free cup of coffee.

Ethan watched someone walk by, eating a Drowzee. The bottom of the vanilla-cake doughnut was dipped in chocolate. *Yum!*

"I think I'll try a Drowzee next time," he said to Devin. "Minus the coffee, I mean."

"Not me. I'm sticking with the Jigglypuff."

*Surprise, surprise,* thought Ethan. His little sister had the world's biggest sweet tooth. *Why would she settle for a half-frosted doughnut when she could have one that was completely frosted?*

He smiled as Devin wiped a streak of pink frosting off her chin with the back of her hand.

"Need a napkin, sweetie?" Dottie approached the table with a paper napkin and a warm smile.

"Looks like the Jigglypuffs taste especially good today."

Devin answered with her mouth full. "They're delicious!"

"I'm glad to hear it. Now, maybe you two can help me choose my next Pokémon-themed doughnut. I'm doing a little survey." Dottie pulled a pencil out from behind her ear. "Which one of these sounds better?" she asked.

Ethan leaned forward so that he could hear her over the buzz of voices outside. People were definitely starting to show up for the lure!

"First choice: I could make a blueberry Squirtle with a chocolate-frosting shell and whipped cream that 'squirts' out of the middle. Get it?"

Devin scrunched up her nose. "That squirting part sounds kind of gross."

Dottie frowned. "You might be right. Well, here's choice number two: the Diglett chocolate-cake pop. Or maybe we'll call it the Dugtrio, and sell three cake pops for the price of two."

Devin bobbed her head up and down. "Yes! That sounds better."

"Wait, there's one more," said Dottie, holding up her hand. "How about the Mankey? That's a powdered-sugar doughnut with banana-cream filling, of course."

"Sold!" said Ethan. "I'll take a dozen—once you've invented them, I mean."

Dottie smiled. "Okay, sounds like one vote for the Dugtrio cake pops and one for the Mankey." She marked something on her notepad and slid the pencil back into her thick, gray hair. "We'll see what the other customers think. Looks like they're finally coming in!"

Sure enough, the bell over her front door was jingling.

And Ethan's and Devin's phones were suddenly buzzing.

"Ugh, it's a Zubat," Ethan said. "That Pokémon stresses me out. I just can't catch things with wings."

"Me neither. That's why I just take its picture," said Devin. Taking photos was her solution for pesky Pokémon. She held up her phone and snapped a photo of the Zubat flapping right over Ethan's head.

When he saw the photo, he ducked. "Yikes! Get that thing away from me."

"Get it yourself," said Devin. "See if you can catch it."

So he tried. Boy, did he try. He flung Poké Balls above, below, and all around that fluttering Zubat. Some of them seemed to go right *through* the Zubat. But none of them captured it. "It's like he's invisible!" said Ethan.

"Who?"

Gianna, Carlo's younger sister, slid into the booth beside them. Her dark curls were pressed against her head, as if she'd just pulled off a bike helmet. "I got here as soon as I could. What did I miss?"

"*You* didn't miss anything," said Ethan. "You could catch this Zubat easily. But I've burned, like, a hundred Poké Balls on it." He tried one more, and then he slid the phone across the table to Gianna. "You try. *Please.*"

Gianna didn't have her own phone, but she often borrowed Devin's or Carlo's to catch Pokémon—and she was the best shot on Team Mystic.

"You just have to center the Pokémon on your screen," she said, as if she were teaching Ethan how to catch a Caterpie. "Then a straight shot should do it." She swiped the Poké Ball, and sure enough, she caught the Zubat on the first try.

Ethan spun sideways in the booth and pretended to bang his head on the window. "Why can't I do it?" he groaned. "I'm a Level-Seven Trainer, and a Gym Defender at two gyms. But I can't catch a stinkin' Zubat."

"You're Level Seven already?" someone asked.

It was Carlo, who was just stepping through the front door. "When you hit Level Eight, you'll get Razz Berries. Then I'll teach you how to sweeten up those annoying Zubat and catch 'em all, no problem."

He was a Level-Thirteen Trainer, so he knew all kinds of Pokémon GO tricks.

"Thanks, Carlo," said Ethan, feeling a little bit better.

When his phone buzzed again, he was happy to see Rattata, a ratlike Pokémon—without wings. He caught it quickly, along with the big-eared Nidoran and furry purple Venonat that the lure brought in.

"Is it just me, or are Weedle getting a whole lot sassier?" asked Devin, trying to catch the springy, wormlike Pokémon on her screen.

"That means you're leveling up," said Ethan. "It's a good thing. Just show those little Larrys who's boss."

Devin laughed—and finally captured the Pokémon. "Larry" was their Dad's nickname for one of his Weedle, so now Ethan and Devin called every Weedle they saw Larry.

Eventually, the pink petals stopped pouring down and the crowd at the doughnut shop thinned out. That's when Dottie hurried over with the survey results.

"The Mankey doughnut wins!" she announced, her gold earrings jingling. "Banana-cream filling it is. I can hardly wait to get started. Come back tomorrow for a sample, okay?"

She rubbed her hands together as she walked back toward the kitchen.

"She seems so happy," said Gianna, as they all stood up to leave. "And I think I know why. Do you want to hear a secret?"

When everyone leaned forward, she said in a hushed voice, "Dottie and Ivan are *dating*."

"What?" Ethan shrunk backward. "But he's her competition!"

Ivan was the owner of an ice cream store across town that had *almost* run Dottie right out of business. Plus, his shop was a rival Pokémon gym. It belonged to Team Valor.

Gianna shrugged. "Who cares? Love is love, I guess."

"And anyway, Dottie's business is doing great," said Devin. "She's even making a Mankey doughnut. You can't do *that* with ice cream."

Carlo cocked his head. "You could make a Mankey banana split, though."

Gianna playfully punched her brother's shoulder. "Don't you dare give Ivan ideas!" she said.

"You steer clear of that ice cream shop. We're on Team Dottie, remember?"

He laughed. "I remember."

"Yeah, we fought hard for this gym," said Ethan, following Carlo out the door. "And if anything ever happens to it, we're stuck training over *there*."

He pointed to the library across the street. It was a Team Mystic gym, too. But the librarian, Mrs. Applegate, didn't allow kids to play Pokémon GO anywhere near the building. So even though Ethan had managed to leave a Spearow in that gym, he could never train it!

Carlo faked a shudder. "You're right. Let's never let anything happen to Dottie's Doughnuts," he said. "Team Dottie it is. Catch you all later!" He waved and took off toward the hardware store, where he was helping out this summer.

While Gianna unlocked her bike from the caterpillar-shaped rack in front of the shop, Ethan stood next to her and tapped his phone screen. The bike rack was also a PokéStop. He spun the Photo Disc and collected two Poké Balls and an egg.

When he heard Mrs. Applegate calling from across the street, he quickly slid his phone back into his pocket.

*How can she bust me for playing?* he wondered.

*I'm not even at the stinking library!*

But Mrs. Applegate didn't have Pokémon on her mind—not at all.

"Have you kids seen Max?" she cried, hurrying into the street without even looking for cars. "My cat got out. He's missing!"

# CHAPTER 2

"**A**re you sure Max isn't still in the library somewhere?" asked Ethan. He had seen the cat once and knew it was pitch-black. A cat that color could easily get lost in the shadowy corners of the old library.

Mrs. Applegate shook her head. "I've looked everywhere. And I shook his can of tuna treats. He *always* comes running for his tuna treats." She held up the plastic container.

"Then I found a hole in the window screen. It's the window Max likes to sit in. So . . . oh, I just *know* he got out. We have to find him!" Her lip started to tremble.

"We'll help you look for him," Devin said sweetly. "We'll look right now."

Ethan nodded. "We can split up. Maybe Devin and I can go one way, and . . ."

"Mrs. Applegate and I can go the other," Gianna bravely volunteered. "We'll meet back here."

Ethan shot her a relieved smile. The truth was, Mrs. Applegate scared him a little. He was happy to partner with Devin and head off in the other direction.

"Maybe Max is in the alley behind the library," he said to Devin. "Follow me."

They searched opposite sides of the alleyway, behind dumpsters and under wooden pallets. When they reached the back door of the library, Ethan looked up at the window. Sure enough, there was a gaping hole in the screen.

"Do you think Max did that?" he asked Devin. "Does he have claws?"

Devin gazed up. "I don't know," she said. "That's a really big hole, though."

What Ethan really wanted to ask was, "Do you think Max will use those claws on us if we try to catch him?"

He didn't ask, because he didn't want his eight-year-old sister to think he was scared of cats.

*But cats are kind of like Zubat,* he admitted to

himself. *They're tough to catch, especially when they don't want to be caught.*

After circling the entire block and a few more alleys, Ethan and Devin came up dry. They hadn't caught a cat, but Ethan had managed to catch a Raticate and two Rattata. He suddenly wondered if there were any *real* rats in those alleyways.

As soon as Devin and Mrs. Applegate rounded the corner in front of the library, Ethan could tell that they hadn't found Max, either.

"What am I going to do?" wailed Mrs. Applegate. "He's never been outside on his own before!"

Dottie must have seen Mrs. Applegate wringing her hands, because she came out of her shop, wiping her own hands on her apron. "What's wrong, honey?" she asked the librarian, as if she were talking to a child who'd dropped her doughnut.

"Max is missing!" said Mrs. Applegate. Tears started to trickle down her wrinkled cheeks.

"Oh, dear," said Dottie. "Don't cry, now. We'll find him. In fact, did you know you have a group of kid detectives right here in your midst?"

*Uh-oh,* thought Ethan. He had the sinking

feeling that Dottie was about to volunteer him and his friends for something.

"Really?" said Mrs. Applegate, dabbing at her eyes.

"Oh, yes," said Dottie. "These kids helped me solve a mystery at my bakery just a couple weeks ago. I bet they'll be able to find Max in no time." She winked at Ethan, then patted Mrs. Applegate's shoulder. "You show them a picture of your cat, and then let them do their thing."

"Yes!" said Devin. "If you have a picture, I can make lost cat posters. I'm good at that."

Ethan wished she hadn't spoken up so quickly, but he had to agree, she was a great poster maker. When Mrs. Applegate hurried into the library to find a photo, he pulled Devin and Gianna into a huddle. "Do we really want to do this?" he asked. "Mrs. Applegate hasn't exactly been friendly to us. She won't even let us train Pokémon at her gym!"

Gianna must have already thought of that, because she said, "Maybe if we do this for her, she'll be a little nicer to us. Don't you think?"

Devin scrunched up her freckled nose. "How can you two think about Pokémon at a time like this? Max is lost—he's all alone out there. We have to find him!"

Gianna looked just as guilty as Ethan suddenly

felt. "You're right, Devin," she said. "We should help Mrs. Applegate and Max. Because it's the right thing to do."

Ethan sighed. "So I guess we're doing this, then?"

When Devin and Gianna nodded, he held out his hand, palm down. "Team Mystic?"

They put their hands on top of his and said, together, "Team Mystic!"

*Let the Mystery of the Missing Cat begin,* thought Ethan.

But when Mrs. Applegate hurried out of the library and showed them a faded photo, Ethan groaned inside. It was a *terrible* photograph.

Her black cat was barely visible against a navy blue sofa. It was like trying to see a Metapod against a bright green bush. *But I guess it's all we have to work with,* he told himself.

As Devin stared at the photo, she chewed her bottom lip. Then she gave Mrs. Applegate a bright smile and said, "We'll make a bunch of posters—a hundred of them. We'll put them all over town, on every PokéStop—er, I mean, on signs and stuff."

Ethan held his breath, wondering if Mrs. Applegate would lecture them about playing Pokémon GO. But she didn't.

"Thank you, dear," she said, patting Devin's

arm. "I'm going to keep looking now. I won't sleep until my boy is back home with me."

As she walked away, her shoulders sagging, Ethan felt a pang of sympathy. *We have to bring Max home,* he decided. *As soon as possible.*

# CHAPTER 3

By dinnertime, Devin had made a tall stack of posters. She had used Mrs. Applegate's photo of Max, but Ethan was happy to see that she'd added something else: an image of the catlike Pokémon Meowth in the corner. *That* would grab people's attention—especially if they hung the sign on PokéStops.

"Can we hang up the signs during our walk tonight?" asked Ethan while they ate.

Thanks to Pokémon GO, his family took a walk every night after dinner. While Ethan and Devin hunted for Pokémon, Mom tried to hatch Pokémon eggs and log steps toward her gold

Jogger medal.

And Dad? Mostly he wandered around bumping into things. Ethan glanced across the table at the bruise on Dad's forehead. The poor guy had walked into a maple tree just last night, hunting for a hard-to-spot Spearow.

Mom had upped the stakes, though. She'd been leading them on walks through *new* parts of town so that they could explore different PokéStops instead of the same old, same old. Then, after the walk, she would say, "Tell me something new that you learned from Pokémon GO today."

Some nights Ethan had to work really hard to answer that question.

*I guess she doesn't want our brains to turn to mush this summer,* he thought as he ate a spoonful of peas.

"Sure, we can hang the posters," she said. "It's sweet that you two are helping Mrs. Applegate find her cat."

"Well, we're going to try," said Ethan. "No promises."

"Hey, can we walk around the school playground tonight?" asked Devin. "It's kind of between the library and Mrs. Applegate's house. Maybe Max started walking back toward his own neighborhood."

Dad helped himself to another piece of chicken. "Sounds smart," he said. "If I were a cat, that's what I'd do."

"And can Gia come, too?" asked Devin.

Mom nodded, but that was no surprise. Gianna came with them on their walks almost every night, and Devin shared her phone with her.

After dinner, everyone piled into the car. On the way to Newville Elementary, they stopped to pick up Gianna, who was wearing her lucky Pokémon-hunting cap. It had two antennae on top, like some of her favorite Bug-type Pokémon.

The backseat felt crowded now, and the antennae of Gia's cap kept bopping Ethan in the forehead. "Gia, can you please control your cap?" he said, only half-kidding as he rubbed his head.

"Oh, sorry!" she said. She laughed and pulled off the cap, resting it safely in her lap.

Finally, they pulled into the school parking lot.

*It's weird to be here during the summer,* thought Ethan as he stepped out of the car. It seemed so quiet without kids buzzing around the red-brick building. And the playground was completely empty.

"Where do you think the PokéStops are?" asked Devin, scanning her phone.

"How should I know?" said Ethan. "Look for

the blue squares."

"Let's walk around the basketball courts first," said Mom. "Then we can come back and search the playground." She was bouncing up and down on the balls of her feet, ready to log some steps.

As they walked, Ethan kept an eye out for Max. Devin was scanning the blacktop, too. He even saw her ignore her vibrating phone while tracking what turned out to be a squirrel in a bush.

When Ethan spotted a Zubat on his phone, his search for Max came to a squeaking, squealing halt.

"Really?" he wanted to holler at the Zubat. "At a time like this?"

He sighed and sat down on a bench. When his phone vibrated *again,* he scolded the Weedle that popped up. "Don't waste my time, Larry. I've got a Zubat to take down."

Then he tried his best to capture the winged Pokémon. He did what Gianna said—he angled his phone until the Zubat was dead center. Then he took the straightest swipe he could with that Poké Ball.

But once again, it seemed to go right *through* the Zubat. *What's up with that?* Ethan wanted to scream.

The Zubat taunted him, screeching like a

prehistoric cockroach.

About twenty more Poké Balls in, the Zubat finally got sucked into a ball. But only for a second.

When it sprang back out again, Ethan groaned. "So you want to play that way, huh? Fine. I don't have time for this."

Then he did something he had never done before. He pressed the run button in the upper left-hand corner of his screen, and he walked away from the Zubat—feeling like a total loser.

*Focus on Max,* Ethan reminded himself.

It helped when Dad suddenly hollered, "Hey, I found a PokéStop!" He was standing in front of a statue of a red fox, the school mascot.

As Ethan stepped toward it, the blue square on his phone turned into a circle. He spun the Photo Disc and collected two Poké Balls and a Revive.

Devin, meanwhile, slid a poster out of her backpack and taped it to the base of the statue. "Do you think it'll stay?" she asked Ethan.

"Maybe with a few more pieces of tape," he said.

"Wait!" said Mom, jogging over. "Did you read the plaque at the bottom? Try to learn something before you cover it up with a cat poster."

Ethan sighed and read it out loud. HOME OF THE NEWVILLE RED FOXES SINCE 1968.

Mom nodded, satisfied. Then they walked on.

"Any sign of Max?" Devin asked Ethan.

He shook his head. "I managed to run away from a Zubat, though. Have I mentioned how much I *hate* Zubat?"

Devin giggled. "Me, too. Maybe we should make T-shirts and start an 'I Hate Zubat' club. But Gia can't join. She's too good at catching them." She jogged ahead to catch up with Gianna.

After a half hour, they had taped posters to a few more PokéStops, including the school sign near the front entrance and a water fountain.

"With all these cat posters, it looks more like MEWville Elementary than Newville Elementary," said Dad, chuckling.

"Good one, Dad!" said Ethan. He liked to support Dad's good jokes, since there were way too many bad ones.

Devin giggled, but Gianna stopped walking and tapped her chin thoughtfully. "That gives me an idea. When you're trying to find a cat, you have to *think* like a cat—or at least like a feline Pokémon. Where would Meowth be hiding?"

"Ooh, I know. Let me check my tracker," said Devin. She tapped the bottom right corner of her phone, where pictures and outlines of all the nearby Pokémon showed up. "Nope. No Meowths around here right now."

"Ouch!"

Everyone turned toward Dad, who had just stubbed his toe on the base of a flagpole.

"Remember to look up while you walk, dear," said Mom. "And maybe you should wear more sensible shoes next time."

Dad always wore his sandals for walks. *With socks,* Ethan thought, and he groaned inside. Not exactly a fashion statement.

But something Mom had said gave Ethan an idea. *Remember to look up,* she'd said. So he glanced up the flagpole. And started to think like a cat.

"Cats climb trees," he said out loud.

Gianna nodded. "They sure do. So where can we find a bunch of trees?"

Ethan and Devin swapped glances. "The nature preserve!" they both said.

Then they raced toward the car. *This night is starting to get a whole lot more interesting,* thought Ethan. *We're going to find that cat yet!*

# CHAPTER 4

"One hour," said Mom, checking the sun's position in the sky. "No later than that, or Dad and I will come looking for you."

"Yes, ma'am," said Ethan. But he could barely wait for the car to come to a stop in the driveway so that they could hop out.

The Pheasant Ranch Nature Preserve was just a few blocks from their house. So as soon as they got home, he, Devin, and Gianna took off running down the street. When a few posters fluttered out of Devin's hands, she hollered at Ethan to slow down already. He tried to. But he couldn't wait to get to the trailhead!

"Tape a poster to the Little Library," said Gianna as they passed a wooden box on a post. The Little Library was a place for neighbors to share books. Plus, it was a PokéStop. So while Devin taped a cat poster to the front door of the library, Ethan spun the Photo Disc and collected a few Poké Balls. He sure needed them, after his recent run-in with the Zubat.

When they reached the trailhead to Pheasant Ranch, which was also a PokéStop, he collected a few more. Then he heard a familiar voice that made his skin crawl.

"What are you guys doing?"

It was Brayden the Great, a neighbor who wasn't exactly a friend. He and his Team Valor friends had tried to take over the gym at Dottie's Doughnuts just a few weeks ago. Ethan had been *so* mad at him!

*We won the gym back,* Ethan reminded himself. *So I should at least try to be nicer to Brayden now.* But it was so hard with a kid who bragged about every Pokémon he caught—and everything his parents bought him. In fact, he was zooming down the street right now on what looked like a brand-new scooter.

"We're just searching for Pokémon," Ethan said, pasting on a smile.

"And we're searching for Mrs. Applegate's lost cat, Max," said Devin, holding up a poster.

*Great,* thought Ethan. *Now Brayden is going to want to look for Max with us.*

But he just took a long look at the poster and shrugged his shoulders. "Haven't seen him. But if you spot any rare Pokémon while you're out looking, make sure to let me know."

"Yeah," said Ethan, as Brayden buzzed away. "We'll be sure . . . *not* to." He waited until the scooter was out of sight before following the girls onto the trail.

Devin stopped for a second to study her phone. "Okay, I'll keep an eye out for Meowth while we look for Max," she said, checking her tracking feature.

"Meowth? I'm holding out for the legendary Mewtwo, or Mew," said Ethan. *Why not aim high?*

Gianna seemed to have something else in mind. As she swatted at a pesky fly, she said, "I'll bet there are a lot of Bug-type Pokémon out here. My favorite!"

But the first Pokémon they found was Vulpix. "Oh, it's so cute," said Devin, holding up her phone. "It looks like a little fox. Kind of like Eevee. I have to take a picture."

Even Ethan had to admit, Vulpix was pretty

cute. He captured it easily and then walked on.

As they got deeper into the woods, the trail suddenly felt squishy under Ethan's feet. Had it rained recently? He studied the ground. "Remember to look up in the trees," he told the girls. "But look down sometimes, too. If Max is out here, maybe he left a trail of paw prints."

"Good idea," said Gianna.

"Speaking of footprints," said Devin, "I think Meowth just popped up in my tracker. Is this an outline of Meowth?"

"Yeah, that's him, I think," said Ethan, studying the gray outline. "Or maybe it's Mew. Wouldn't it be great if we found Max *and* Mew out here?"

He nearly ran into Gianna, who had dropped low to study the ground. "This might sound crazy," she said, "but I think I just found cat prints. Take a look."

Ethan stepped around her, careful not to smear the prints.

Devin hurried over, too. "Hey, those *do* look like cat prints!" she said.

"Or coyote tracks," said Ethan. He immediately regretted it.

"There are coyotes out here?" said Devin, glancing over her shoulder. "How do you know?"

"Dad told me once," said Ethan. "But they

won't bother us. Don't worry."

Devin's green eyes widened. "I'm not worried about *us*," she countered. "I'm worried about Max."

*Oh,* thought Ethan. *Right.*

"If you're worried about Max, let's follow these paw prints," said Gianna. "Maybe we'll get lucky and find him."

So they set off tracking the prints, which very quickly took them off the trail.

"We should stick to the main path," said Ethan, even though he was dying to know where the prints led.

Devin sighed. "We've come this far. Can't we go just a little farther? Max needs us! What if he gets attacked by a coyote?" As the sun sank behind a tree, she shivered.

Ethan checked the time. "We only have half an hour left," he said. "How about if we follow the trail for ten minutes? Then we have to hurry back."

Devin agreed, and Gianna was already racing off into the bushes.

The ground got softer and softer beneath their feet, which made tracking the prints easy. Until they disappeared into a tuft of mossy grass.

"Where'd he go next?" asked Gianna, looking up.

"Maybe toward those trees," said Devin,

pointing ahead. "Let's go see."

As they wandered through the dense thicket of trees, she called softly for the cat. "Here, Maxie. Here, kitty, kitty."

"We're running out of trees," said Gianna eventually. "This looks kind of like a marsh."

As Ethan felt wetness seep into his shoes, he jumped backward. "I think it *is* a marsh. Let's go back."

He turned to lead the way. He pushed through the bushes and trees, waiting for the moment when they'd pop out and find the trail again. But that moment didn't come.

"Do you know where you're going?" Devin finally asked.

Ethan wanted to lie to her, but the truth was, he was starting to get nervous. "Let me check my GPS," he said, pulling out his phone.

When he saw the words "No Signal," his nervousness turned into full-blown panic. "Do either of you have a signal?" he asked.

Devin's voice sounded strained when she said, "Nope."

"I do!" said Gianna. "Wait, no, it's gone. Let's keep walking until I get it back."

Ethan spun in a slow circle. "I don't even know which way to go," he admitted. "And is it just me, or is it getting dark?"

As they all looked up at the sky, they heard a faint yipping sound in the distance.

Devin gripped Ethan's arm. "Is that . . . a coyote?"

# CHAPTER 5

Ethan's heart was in his throat. But he took a deep breath and tried to stay calm for his little sister's sake.

"It's not a coyote," he said, sounding more sure than he actually felt. "It's probably Brayden's golden retriever. Now, let's think for a second. Which way is the sun setting?"

Devin chewed her bottom lip and looked up. "That way." She pointed to the left.

"So that's west," said Ethan. "The sun sets in the west." He wasn't sure what to do with that information, but at least it was a start.

"Good," said Gianna. "Our neighborhood is

west of Pheasant Ranch, isn't it? At least I think it is. Let me check my phone. Oh, right—no signal. Wait . . . I think I've got one now!"

She ran up ahead, holding her phone toward the sky. "Yes, a signal!"

Ethan and Devin raced after her, and finally she was able to pull up her Pokémon GO map.

"So this green blob is the conservancy, and the blue must be the marsh we nearly walked into. There's a bunch of PokéStops—that must be our neighborhood. Follow me."

They pushed through the thicket until finally, *finally,* they were back on the actual trail. Ethan felt relief wash over his body like rain.

When they heard the sound of bike tires coming toward them, he felt even better.

The boy in the yellow T-shirt riding the bike looked familiar. "Wyatt?" said Ethan. He hadn't seen Wyatt since school ended. He looked a lot more tan—and when he hopped off his bike, he seemed like he'd grown an inch or two.

"Hey, what are you guys doing way out here?" asked Wyatt, wheeling his bike toward them.

"Tracking paw prints," said Gianna, pointing toward the ground.

"You're tracking him, too?" said Wyatt. "I've been looking for that little guy all night. Team

Instinct—I mean, my friends and I—are forming a big search party tomorrow. You can join us if you want."

"Really?" said Ethan. "Um, okay. After church, Mom might let us."

"Good! See you later, then." Wyatt hopped back on his bike and pedaled off.

"So much for this being a Team Mystic mystery," said Ethan as Wyatt disappeared around a bend in the trail.

"That's okay," Gianna said brightly. "Team Instinct is alright."

"Yeah, and the more people looking for Max, the better," added Devin.

"True," said Ethan. When his phone buzzed, he glanced down and was surprised to see a yellow tower pop up.

"Hey, there's a gym nearby! Looks like Team Instinct has control of it. Too bad there's no time for a battle right now."

"Maybe tomorrow?" said Gianna. She loved a good Pokémon battle, too.

"Tomorrow," said Ethan. "Let's get going."

On the way home from church, Dad drove by the

library so that Ethan and Devin could check in on Mrs. Applegate. She looked like she hadn't slept a wink, which meant that Max was still missing—they knew it before she even said so.

"We'll find him soon," said Devin. "I have a good feeling about it!"

"I hope so, sweetie," said Mrs. Applegate, taking a big sip from her coffee mug. "My house—and this big old library—sure feel empty without him."

After Ethan and Devin piled back into the car, Dad drove around the block to head home, which led them by a church with an interesting sign out front.

"Hey, look," he said, slowing down to read the sign. "It says PokéStop here. Come one, come all. It's a PokéStop church! Maybe next Sunday, we could—"

"Don't even think about it," said Mom. "Keep driving, mister."

In the backseat, Ethan smothered a smile. Dad was into Pokémon GO as much as he and Devin were, but Mom had a way of squashing his enthusiasm like a bug.

*Poor Dad,* thought Ethan. *Too bad he can't come to the nature preserve with us this afternoon.*

But as he checked the clouds outside the car window, he started to wonder if the whole adventure was going to get rained out.

By the time they got home from church, there were droplets of water starting to splat on the car windows.

"You two should probably stay out of the rain," said Mom, carrying her purse into the house.

"It's just misting!" said Ethan, holding out his hands. *A really wet mist,* he decided, wiping his hands on his pants.

"Bring your umbrellas," said Mom. "And wear your rain boots."

Devin heaved a deep sigh. "It's impossible to catch Pokémon when you're carrying an umbrella," she said, pushing past Ethan to get into the house first.

But Ethan was glad they got to go at all.

By the time they met Gianna at the trailhead, the sun was peeking out from behind a cloud. So there was hope.

There were also a lot of kids wearing yellow T-shirts poking around the trail. *Team Instinct?* wondered Ethan. *Wow, these kids are organized. Matching T-shirts and everything.*

Wyatt sped by on his bike, barely slowing down to talk. "I spotted some tracks by the bridge," he said. "Come check them out!"

With that, he was gone again.

"Is the bridge over by where we were last night?" asked Devin, pausing to think.

"Yup," said Ethan. "It's by the Team Instinct gym, too." He could hardly wait to try his luck against the rival gym. "Let's run!"

That was easier said than done in rain boots. But they made it to the bridge pretty quickly. Ethan only wiped out in the mud once—and managed to pass it off as an intentional slide.

A whole crowd of Team Instinct kids were gathered by the bridge, and they were all looking down.

"Did you find paw prints?" asked Devin, pushing her way through the crowd.

"We sure did," said a girl with a long brown ponytail. "Look—right here." She pointed to the line of muddy tracks crossing the bridge.

"Max is around here somewhere. I know he is!" said Devin, her eyes flashing.

"Wait, who's Max?" asked the Team Instinct girl, standing back up.

"The lost cat!" said Devin. "The one we're all looking for."

"Huh?" The girl cocked her head. "We're not tracking a cat. We're tracking a *fox*. We're trying to help the nature preserve track how many red foxes are left in the area."

*A fox?* Ethan's stomach sank.

"But those are cat tracks, aren't they?" he asked, pointing.

It was Wyatt who knelt beside the prints and explained it all to Ethan. "Cat paw prints don't have these long claw marks at the tips. See? That's a fox, for sure."

"Oh." Ethan was not only disappointed. He also felt a little bit dumb.

When the rain started to fall again, everything felt gray and bleak. Ethan could hardly stand to look at Devin's face. She wore her disappointment like a mask.

Then he remembered something that brightened the world back up again—or at least brightened his Pokémon GO map. The yellow Team Instinct gym!

"Mind if I stop for a battle?" he asked Devin.

She shrugged. "I'll hold the umbrella so you don't get your phone wet."

"Thanks," he said. Sometimes his sister was alright. She and Gianna even cheered his Pidgeotto on as it won the first match against a Team Instinct Poliwag.

"Hey, you'll never believe what I'm battling next!" he said to Devin, showing her his phone.

It was a little red Vulpix with a super-fluffy tail.

*Leave it to Team Instinct to leave a foxlike Pokémon in the conservancy gym,* he thought.

The Vulpix seemed too cute to attack—until it released its Flame Charge. Ethan could almost feel the heat as he dodged the fiery blast.

"Attack, Pidgeotto!" he said, tapping the screen. "What are you waiting for?"

Then he felt Devin hitting his arm. "Stop that," he barked at her. "Can't you see that I'm trying to concentrate?"

"Ethan, look!" she whispered loudly in his ear. "Look *now.*"

He tore his eyes away from his screen, and he was sure glad he did.

Standing just a few feet away in a thicket of trees and bushes was a wild animal.

And this was no Pokémon.

It was a real live, really *red* fox.

# CHAPTER 6

"You should have seen it, Carlo," Gianna told her brother. "That fox was better than anything in the Pokédex. Show him the picture you took, Devin."

They were sitting on Gianna and Carlo's porch, watching the rain fall. And all Ethan could think about was the fox they'd just seen.

"We were so close to it," he told Carlo. "I could have reached out and touched it."

"You sure were," Carlo said, studying the photograph. "It's a great picture. You could be a nature photographer, Devin!"

She blushed as she took her phone back. "I'm

disappointed that we didn't find Max, but the fox was pretty special. And what Team Instinct is doing is important, too. Did you know there aren't as many foxes in the forest as there used to be?"

"I didn't know that," said Carlo.

"Hey, when Mom asks tonight what you learned from Pokémon GO, you'll finally have something to say!" said Ethan with a grin.

"Yeah," said Devin. "But when Mrs. Applegate asks if we found Max, we'll have to tell her no." She slumped in the porch swing. "How are we going to look for him in the rain?"

Ethan shrugged. "It's definitely raining now. There's nothing misty about it." He watched the waterfall pouring out of the downspout into the flowerbed below.

"Maybe we can wait it out," said Gianna.

So they tried.

After an hour, Devin had designed a fox-crossing poster on her phone using a picture of Vulpix. And Carlo had taught Ethan how to evolve Eevee, another foxlike Pokémon, into a Vaporeon.

"So if I just nickname it Rainer, it'll evolve into a Vaporeon instead of Flareon or Jolteon?" asked Ethan.

"Yep," said Carlo. "If you want a Jolteon like mine, you nickname your Eevee Sparky."

*Cool!* thought Ethan. He didn't mind rainy days so much if they meant Carlo would be home to teach him a few things.

But as Ethan and Devin made a mad dash through the rain toward their own home, Ethan remembered Max.

*By tomorrow, Max will have been missing for two days,* he realized. *That cat is going to be really hungry. And really wet!*

Ethan woke up to the peaceful sound of . . . silence. No more raindrops falling on the rooftop. *Yes!*

"Can we go hunt for Max?" he asked Mom when he was only halfway into the kitchen.

"Just for a bit this morning," she said. "It's family yard work day, remember? Dad's taking off work this afternoon to help."

"Okay," said Ethan, grabbing a piece of toast from the plate on the table. "Devin, c'mon!"

"Let the girl eat her breakfast," said Mom, shaking her head.

"No time," said Ethan, pulling on his shoes. "We've got very important Team Mystic business."

"Breakfast is important, too," said Mom. "Sit your butt down." She pointed at a chair until Ethan had no choice but to go over and sit in it.

*Sometimes grown-ups are so unreasonable,* he thought with a sigh. But orange juice did taste good.

A half hour later, he, Devin, and Gianna were out in the sunshine, biking toward the library. Hopefully, Mrs. Applegate had good news about Max, but if not, Team Mystic was back on the case.

"Look, it's Dottie," said Gianna, pointing.

Sure enough, Dottie was walking toward them. But she wasn't alone. She was holding hands with a man who looked suspiciously like Ivan.

"They both close their shops on Mondays," said Gianna, giggling. "Aren't they cute?"

Ethan noticed that Dottie looked especially fancy today, in a lavender dress and wide-brimmed hat that set off her brown eyes and skin.

Ivan wore a cap, too, which he tipped toward them as he came closer. "Morning, kids," he said in his thick accent. "Isn't it a beautiful day?"

"Um, yeah," said Ethan, trying not to look at Ivan's bushy eyebrows. They reminded him of long white Caterpie.

"Where were you all yesterday?" asked Dottie. "I had three Mankey doughnuts set aside especially for you."

"Oh, no!" said Devin. "We totally forgot."

"Actually, we were searching for Max in the morning," Ethan explained.

"And stuck in the rain all afternoon," said Gianna.

"Oh, I see," said Dottie. "Well maybe I can pick your brains for a moment about a couple of other doughnuts I was considering."

"Sure. Which ones?" said Ethan. It was always fun to talk doughnuts—almost as much fun as it was to *eat* them.

He was surprised when Dottie pulled her phone out of her purse and brought up a photo of a Caterpie.

"Dottie, have you been playing Pokémon GO?" asked Devin, her eyes wide.

Dottie brushed Devin's question away with a wave of her hand. "Just doing a little research here and there," she said. But she sounded embarrassed, as if she'd just been busted.

"So I'm thinking about baking a key-lime Caterpie. What do you think?"

Devin scrunched up her nose.

"What is it, sweetie?" asked Dottie. "Be honest, now."

"Well," said Devin, "I just don't want to feel like I'm eating a caterpillar."

Ethan agreed. Mostly, though, he wished they'd

stop talking about caterpillars so he wouldn't be tempted to sneak a peek at Ivan's eyebrows.

"Okay, okay, fair enough," said Dottie. "How about a Clefairy cream puff, then? Picture it: a swirl of pink frosting on top, and whipped-cream filling in the middle."

"Yes!" said Gianna. "Now you're talking."

"Ooh, I have the perfect photo for a poster," said Devin. "Remember that one I took of a Clefairy on a soda can?" she asked Ethan.

He did remember—he'd been the one holding the soda.

"The Clefairy cream puff is a great idea," he said to Dottie. "We give it three thumbs up."

Ivan smiled proudly at Dottie and said, "Isn't she creative? I wish I could hire her at the ice cream shop. So far, the only Pokémon ice cream toppings I've been able to come up with are Stardust Sprinkles."

"You can't hire her!" said Devin. "I mean, she's already got a job."

"I certainly do," said Dottie. "And you kids make it a whole lot easier—and more fun." She blew Devin a kiss before heading down the sidewalk with Ivan.

"Let's get going," said Ethan, leaning forward on his bike. "Mrs. Applegate will be opening the library any minute now."

They pedaled around the corner just as Mrs. Applegate was disappearing inside. She caught a glimpse of them coming and turned around with her hands clasped together. "Did you find him?" she asked, her eyes wide behind her glasses.

Ethan barely had the heart to tell her no.

"But we're going to keep looking!" said Devin.

Even Devin sounded a little less hopeful today than she did yesterday, Ethan noticed. *And when Devin starts to lose hope, that's a bad sign.*

"So . . . where do you want to look?" he asked the girls as they biked on.

Devin shrugged. "I don't know. I'm running out of ideas."

Gianna wasn't, though. "How about near the lake?" she said. "Max must be hungry by now. Maybe he headed there looking for fish."

"Yeah, but cats don't really swim," said Ethan. "And it's not like he's got a little kitty fishing pole."

"Well, do you have any better ideas?" asked Devin.

*She's got me there,* he thought. He shook his head, and they set off for the lake.

They'd only gone about two blocks when Ethan heard the buzz of an electric scooter. Brayden pulled up right alongside their bikes. "Hey," he said. "How's your search for the missing cat?"

"Not so great," Ethan mumbled.

"Well, I've got good news for you," he said. "Someone spotted a black cat in the Newville Cemetery. I'll bet you anything it's Max. You should go there and look!"

"Really?" said Devin.

"You're kidding!" said Gianna. "That's *great* news. We'll head over there right now."

Ethan felt a rush of excitement, too, but he held his breath until Brayden was gone. Then he said, "Brayden the Great really creeps me out when he's actually nice to us."

"I know," said Gianna. "It's not natural. But don't think about him right now. We've got a cat to rescue." She took off on her bike, following Devin.

"Right," said Ethan. "Hey, wait for me!"

# CHAPTER 7

"Max is at the cemetery. I know he is!" shouted Devin as they tore down the road on their bikes.

"Slow down!" called Gianna. "My bike's not as fast as yours!"

But Devin was on a mission. Even Ethan was afraid he couldn't keep up with his little sister.

The Newville Cemetery was all the way over by the lake. *We probably should have checked in with Mom before taking off across town,* he told himself as he pedaled. *But good luck telling Devin to turn around now.*

"What kind of Pokémon do you think we'll

find in the graveyard?" he asked Gianna, who was biking by his side. "A Gastly, maybe? Or a Haunter?"

She grinned. "Probably just a bunch of Zubat."

"No!" groaned Ethan. "Don't even say that."

She stuck her tongue out at him and turned on a burst of speed, zooming ahead.

When they got to the cemetery, Devin rode around it in a circle, searching for a bike rack.

"Let's just lock our bikes up against the iron gate," Ethan suggested. He hopped off and showed Devin how.

"It's so quiet," she whispered, taking off her bike helmet. "No wonder Max is hiding out here. It's as quiet as the library."

Ethan almost told her not to get her hopes up—that they didn't know for *sure* that Max was here. But it was so nice to see his little sister hopeful again. He didn't want to be the one to burst her bubble.

As he and Gianna followed Devin through the gates, he pulled out his phone.

*We're looking for Max,* he reminded himself. *But if there happens to be a Gastly floating around, I'm gonna grab it.*

After one lap of the cemetery, Ethan was surprised to find zero Pokémon. But there were

PokéStops *everywhere*—statues of saints and stone benches dedicated to people who had passed away.

After Ethan spun a Photo Disc of an angel statue and collected his rewards, he was surprised to see his screen flash.

"Level up!" it said, along with a brilliant, white number eight.

"Yes!" Ethan pumped his fist. "I made it. I'm a Level-Eight Trainer."

He checked his inventory and was thrilled to see not just one Razz Berry, but ten of them. And now that he had those berries, he wanted to use them.

"Where are all the Pokémon?" he called to the girls.

Devin shushed him. "There probably aren't any hiding here, because of . . . you know, the *people*." She pointed toward the ground.

"Huh?"

She sighed with exasperation. "You may be older than me, Ethan, but sometimes you're not very smart."

"I think what Devin is trying to say is that it wouldn't be respectful to hunt Pokémon in a graveyard," said Gianna. "Right, Devin?"

"Exactly. Thank you, Gia. Besides, we're supposed to be hunting for Max, remember?"

Ethan still didn't get it. *Why have all these PokéStops here if there aren't any Pokémon?*

But he tried to keep his voice down and his thoughts to himself as he searched under benches and around tombstones for a runaway black cat.

When the search turned up nothing, Ethan checked the clock on his phone. "Devin, we really gotta go," he said. "It's almost time for family yard work day."

Just saying the words made his back hurt. There was nothing worse than leaning over a garden pulling weeds when what you *really* wanted to be doing was hunting for cats and Gastly!

"Already?" whined Devin. "But Max is here somewhere. I know he is!"

While she took one more quick lap around a large tomb at the end of the graveyard, Ethan sat down on the nearest bench.

"You've said that before," he mumbled, more to himself than to her. "And you've been wrong before. Maybe he *was* here, but he's moved on by now."

As soon as the words were out of Ethan's mouth, he heard something.

"What was that?" he asked, holding his breath.

Then he heard it again. A low, throaty meow. It was *almost* a growl.

And it was coming from beneath the bench that Ethan was sitting on.

Oh so slowly, Ethan stood up and turned around. He squatted low—and came face to face with a very big, very black cat.

With his chewed-up ear and matted fur, Max looked like he'd had a rough couple of days. He scooted backward under the bench and growled.

"Here, boy. It's okay. I won't hurt you." Ethan offered his outstretched hand.

*Hisssss!* The cat puffed up, showing some very sharp teeth. Then he lunged forward.

"Yikes!" Ethan stumbled backward and fell on his butt.

The cat sprang past him and took off across the cemetery.

"It's him. It's Max!" Ethan jumped up and hollered for the girls. "Get him!"

"Where?" Devin spun around.

Gianna caught sight of the cat and started chasing him, but that only made Max run faster.

"I'll get him!" cried Ethan, racing around the edge of the cemetery to cut Max off at the pass. But just before their paths crossed, Ethan tripped over a flowerpot and landed sprawled in the grass.

The last thing he saw was Max disappearing through the iron gate of the graveyard.

# CHAPTER 8

"Oh, no," said Devin, sinking onto the ground beside Ethan. "We might have just lost our big chance to catch Max."

"No, we didn't," said Gianna, running toward them. "We just need to come back later with something to lure Max toward us. Tuna fish maybe! Remember how Mrs. Applegate said he likes tuna treats?"

"Yeah. Do you think that'll work?" Devin asked, looking up at Gianna with hopeful eyes.

"Sure I do," said Gianna. "The main thing is, we found Max. And he's okay."

*Sort of,* Ethan wanted to say. He was afraid to

tell the girls about Max's chewed-up ear. *Maybe he did have a run-in with a coyote,* he thought with a shiver.

"But what if Mom doesn't let us come back here later?" Devin asked.

Ethan sighed. "She might not. This is kind of far from home, and she doesn't like us biking at night—not without an adult."

"I have an idea," said Gianna. "Carlo is babysitting me tonight while Mom works. Maybe you could stay at our house, and Carlo could go with us to the cemetery. He's fourteen, which is *kind* of like an adult."

"Yeah," said Ethan. "That might work." *And it'd be cool to hang out with Carlo.*

But first? Family yard work day. *Ugh.*

So after looking for Max one last time in the grass beyond the gates, they climbed onto their bikes and headed for home.

"This is such a waste of time," said Ethan. He was crouched over a tomato plant, so his voice came out muffled.

"What is?" asked Devin, taking a bite out of a crisp peapod.

"Hey!" Ethan sat back upright and pointed his finger. "You're supposed to be *weeding* the garden—not eating it."

Devin shrugged and pulled another peapod off the vine. "I need energy to do yard work. What's a waste of time?"

"Weeding a garden that's just going to have more weeds in it tomorrow," he said. "What's wrong with weeds, anyway? Some people eat dandelions. Did you know that they're weeds?"

Devin shook her head. "Did you learn that from Pokémon GO?" she asked, giggling.

"I wish," said Ethan. "What I *really* wish is that we could set a lure here in the garden so that while we weed, the Pokémon would come to us. That would at least make family yard work day more interesting."

"Yeah," said Devin. "But Mom would kill us. So that would be kind of a waste of time, too."

"I guess." Ethan bent back over the tomato plant, and then he popped back up.

"Wait a minute," he said. "I think I earned a lure module when I hit Level Eight." He pulled his phone out of his pocket, checking first to make sure Mom and Dad were still trimming trees on the other side of the yard. Then he checked his items.

"Yes, I do have a lure!"

"Ethan, you can't use that right now," Devin scolded. "I already told you—Mom will kill you. We're supposed to be working. And besides, you can only place those at PokéStops."

"I'm not going to use it now," he said. "I was thinking we could set it at the graveyard tonight to try to draw in some Pokémon."

"Oh."

*So take that, Miss Pea Eater,* Ethan wanted to say.

"But if you set a lure, then lots of people will come to the cemetery. And they'll scare Max away!"

Ethan hesitated. Devin was right—he knew she was. He hated it when that happened.

"Okay, then, how about some incense?" he said. "That would lure Pokémon toward us, but no one else would see it."

"That's a good idea," said Devin.

"Yeah," said Ethan. "It's brilliant. Except I happen to be fresh out of incense." He sighed and reached for another weed.

The next hour stretched into two, and after a lemonade break, into almost *three* hours.

"Is it ever going to end?" grumbled Ethan as he pulled yet another thistle out of the ground.

"Probably not," said Devin. "Probably never."

Then they heard a yelp from Dad. He was using a weed trimmer around the base of a tree.

"Are you hurt?" Ethan heard Mom call.

"No," said Dad. And then he mumbled something about a Spearow.

"Hey, are you playing Pokémon GO?" asked Ethan, standing up to look. "No fair!"

"Not a Spearow," said Dad, wiping something off his head. "A *sparrow*. A real-live sparrow just pooped on my head."

Ethan nearly choked on his laughter. He could tell that Mom was fighting back giggles, too. And Devin didn't even try. She was laughing like crazy, rolling around in the dirt like a wobbly Weedle. Everyone thought the sparrow incident was the funniest thing ever—except for Dad.

He ran into the house to get a tissue. And *that* was pretty much the end of family yard work day. Hurrah!

But the sparrow that Ethan thought was a Spearow had just given him an idea. He pulled off his work gloves and started jogging toward the house.

"Devin, come on!"

He waited until they were safely in his room before he shut the door and told her his plan.

"Remember how I said that the gym at the

library is pretty much worthless?"

Devin shrugged. "Yeah, I guess."

"Well, I was wrong," said Ethan. "I still have a Pokémon at that gym—my Spearow. And any time you leave a Pokémon at a gym, you get a Gym Defender bonus."

Devin's ears perked up at the sound of that.

"I have a Pokémon at Dottie's gym," she reminded him. "I left my Pidgeot there."

"Right," said Ethan. "So every day or so, you and I each get a Defender bonus—Stardust and PokéCoins to spend in the shop!"

"What?" said Devin, her jaw dropping. "Why has no one ever told me this before?"

Ethan shrugged. "I don't know—because we're pretty new at this, and we probably don't have *that* many coins to spend yet. But maybe we have enough for incense to use at the cemetery tonight. Let's check!"

They grabbed their phones and clicked on the "Shop" icon.

"There," said Ethan. "See the shield in the top right corner? Mine has the number two in it, because I left two Pokémon at gyms—one at Dottie's and one at the library. Yours has a number one, for your Pidgeot."

"Yeah, but how many PokéCoins do we have?"

asked Devin. She tapped on the shield and nearly fell off the bed. "A hundred and twenty PokéCoins? Whoa, I'm rich!"

Ethan didn't tell her that he had twice that amount—and six thousand Stardust. He felt pretty rich, himself.

*Take that, Moneybags Brayden with the fat allowance!* he thought with a grin. *I have plenty of PokéCoins to buy incense.*

He could hardly wait to get to the cemetery and *use* it.

# CHAPTER 9

"Do you have the tuna?" asked Ethan as soon as they got to Gianna and Carlo's house.

Gianna nodded, pointing to her backpack. "I packed two cans, just in case."

"We've got something, too," said Ethan. "But it's a surprise—if Devin doesn't spill the beans."

His little sister wasn't a great secret keeper. At that very moment, she looked like a bouncy Weedle ready to burst out of a Poké Ball. So he gave her his best grown-up look—the one that said, *If you don't play by the rules, you'll pay.*

She grinned at him and pretended to zip her lips, lock them, and throw away the key.

"Are you guys ready to do this?" asked Carlo, skipping down the porch stairs. He looked like he was dressed for a serious mission, sporting black biker gloves and a jacket with rolled-up sleeves.

Ethan looked down at his own clothes: the blue T-shirt that he'd once thought was so cool, and his baggier-than-baggy shorts.

He yanked up his shorts a bit and sighed. *Oh, well. Maybe when I'm using my incense at the cemetery, Carlo won't notice what I'm wearing.*

As Carlo wheeled his bike out from the garage, Ethan saw a wire cage strapped to the back.

"What's that for?" he asked.

"It's our old bunny cage," said Carlo. "It'll help us catch Max and bring him home, safe and sound."

"I never thought about how we were going to hang on to Max once we found him," Ethan admitted.

*That's why Carlo is the Team Mystic Gym Leader,* he reminded himself. *And pretty much the coolest guy I know.*

The bike ride across town felt longer this time. Maybe it was because Ethan *knew* that Max was in the cemetery—or had been. They actually had a chance at catching him. And with the incense, Ethan had a good chance of catching some

Pokémon, too!

When they reached the cemetery gates, the sun had slid behind a cloud. The graveyard looked dark and gloomy.

"A little purple incense will brighten this place right up," Ethan whispered to Devin as he pulled out his phone.

She clamped her hand over her mouth. "Are you going to do it now?" she whispered.

He nodded as he opened his items and clicked on the incense. "But don't tell Gianna and Carlo yet. Let's wait and see if it works, first."

The incense appeared on his map almost instantly. A thin plume of purple smoke began circling Ethan's Trainer avatar. The screen suddenly jumped into night mode, and with that purple ring of smoke in the middle of it, it looked dark and mysterious.

Ethan showed Devin, whose eyes grew wide. "Spooky," she said.

Up ahead, Gianna was pulling something out of her backpack. "Hey, what should we do with the tuna?" she called to Carlo, who was in the lead. "Should we open it now, or wait till we see Max?"

"He might come running when he hears the sound of the can opening," said Carlo. "Let's try it now."

Gianna set the can down on a cement bench. When she pulled back the tab, the sound cut through the stillness of the cemetery.

Ethan covered his ears and pretended to wince. "If there are any cats within a mile of this place, they heard that can opening!" he said to Devin.

But no cats came running.

"Now what?" asked Gianna. "This tuna fish kind of stinks."

"Let's put it in the cage," said Carlo. "Maybe Max will come for it when we're not so close by." He carried the wire cage over and placed the tuna inside. "Now, let's walk away for a while. Didn't you say there were some PokéStops around here?"

Gianna nodded. "Follow me."

She led them all in a giant loop around the cemetery, passing every PokéStop to collect Poké Balls. Near one statue, Ethan saw Devin checking the tracking feature on her phone.

"Do you see Pokémon?" he whispered. "Is the incense working?"

"You won't believe it," she said. She showed him the phone, and there was the gray silhouette of a cat—a cat standing up on his hind legs, just like a human.

"Mewtwo?" Ethan whispered.

"Probably just Meowth," said Devin. "He's

more common."

"Or maybe Mew!" said Ethan. They were all catlike Pokémon who stood on their hind legs. Why couldn't it be the legendary Mewtwo or the mythical Mew?

"Wait, you see a Pokémon?" asked Gianna. "I thought there weren't any here."

"Well, it's possible that Ethan *might* have used a little incense," said Devin, giggling.

"You did?" said Carlo. "Nice move, Ethan. Hopefully it'll work on Max, too, if the tuna fish doesn't."

Ethan walked a little taller after hearing Carlo's compliment. But he stuck close to Devin, because that girl knew how to track a Pokémon's footsteps. And if Mew was somewhere in the cemetery, Ethan wanted in on that action.

As Devin tiptoed toward a far corner of the graveyard, Ethan followed right on her heels. A tall tomb rose toward the sky, blocking what little light was coming from the cloud-covered sun. He tried not to think about what was inside the tomb.

"Two footsteps!" Devin whispered. "We're getting closer to Meowth."

"You mean Mew," whispered Ethan, grinning.

She kept walking, past crumbling headstones in what looked like a very old part of the cemetery.

"He's here somewhere!" she said.

But at that moment, Gianna called from the opposite corner of the graveyard. "Ethan! Devin! Get over here—we found Max!"

"They found Max?" said Ethan. "Right now? But we're about to capture Mew!"

Devin shrugged. "Max is more important than Mew," she said. "I mean, think about it: Max is *real.* Come on!"

Ethan reluctantly followed her toward the front of the cemetery. But all he could think was, *If we're not going to chase down Mew, then that incense was an epic waste of my PokéCoins.*

"He's sniffing the tuna," whispered Gianna, ducking down behind a headstone. "Look!"

Ethan glanced to his left and saw the big black cat near the cage. He stood on his hind legs, like Mew, with his front paws on the edge of the bench. And he sniffed that wire cage as if it held the most delicious meal in the world.

"He's going for it!" said Ethan.

"So am I," whispered Devin. She crept toward the cat and slowly raised her phone. Ethan saw a flashing light as she snapped her photo.

Max saw it, too. He took off like a shot into the heart of the cemetery.

"Devin!" everyone hollered at once.

But they didn't have to say another word. Her face crumpled. "I'm sorry," she said, her cheek quivering. "I'm so used to taking pictures of Pokémon. I just . . . I'm sorry."

She sunk down onto the bench next to the cage.

"Can't we try again?" asked Gianna. "Should we walk away?"

Carlo shrugged. "We can try. But Max might be on to us now."

Ethan crossed his fingers while they started to circle the cemetery again. He was hoping that Max would return. But he was *also* hoping they'd have another run-in with Mew.

While the others walked from PokéStop to PokéStop, Ethan walked directly toward the tall tomb in the farthest corner of the cemetery. He checked his phone every few seconds, hoping to see the gray silhouette of a cat.

As he passed the tomb, he held his breath. But his phone stayed silent in his hand. No buzzing. No catlike Pokémon in the app's tracking feature, either.

So he kept walking. He watched the ground carefully, trying not to trip over an old headstone. The sun was setting. It was almost dark as Ethan circled the tomb. And that's when he heard it.

A long, low moan rose from the earth.

It sounded like the wind through the trees on an October night.

*But it's July,* thought Ethan. *And there's not a tree in sight.*

The hair stood up on his arms, and a cool shiver ran down his spine.

# CHAPTER 10

Ethan cocked his head, listening carefully. There it was again—an eerie moan, louder this time. It was getting closer!

In a flash, Ethan took off running, as if a Zubat were swooping after him through the dark cemetery. He dodged headstones, tripped over flowerpots, rounded a statue, and finally ran straight into his friends.

He was so out of breath, he could barely tell them what he'd heard. And as the words came out of his mouth, they sounded so silly—he knew they did!

"You heard a what, now? A *moan*?" asked Gianna.

"Are you sure it wasn't the wind?" asked Carlo. The corner of his mouth twitched, as if he was fighting a smile.

*Great,* thought Ethan. *Just when the guy was starting to respect me a little.*

"Never mind," he said, quickly changing the subject. "Did Max ever come back?"

Carlo shook his head. "And it's getting pretty late now. We should probably go."

Ethan didn't have to be told twice. After the moaning incident, he didn't care if he ever set foot in the cemetery again—Max or no Max.

He practically had to drag Devin away from the cement bench, though. She kept looking over her shoulder, as if Max might suddenly appear.

When they finally reached the front entrance, Ethan was surprised to see the gate closed. "Wasn't that open when we got here?" he asked.

"Yeah," said Carlo. "It sure was." He pulled on the handle of the gate, tugging it backward. Then he tried pushing it forward. "I don't believe it," he whispered.

"What?" asked Ethan, his voice cracking.

Carlo tried slipping his hand through the bars, but he couldn't reach the handle in front. As he pulled his hand back through, he turned to face Ethan.

"What?" Ethan asked again in a tiny voice.

Carlo took a deep breath. "The groundskeeper must have come through and not seen us. We're, um . . . we're locked in."

The words hung in the air for just a moment.

Then Devin started to whimper.

Ethan turned around to comfort her, but he was surprised to see that she wasn't crying. She was nervously chewing on a fingernail.

Standing beside her, Gianna looked worried, but she wasn't the whimpering type.

Ethan strained his ears, and then he heard it again. There was someone else in the cemetery with them—he was sure of it. And this time, he was determined to get to the bottom of it.

He used the flashlight on his phone and walked toward the nearest row of headstones. "Who's there?" he called, wishing his voice would stop wobbling. "Come out and show your face!"

The tougher Ethan talked, the tougher he felt. But when someone jumped up from behind a headstone, he shrieked and fell backward. He landed hard and then fumbled around in the grass, looking for his phone.

When he found it, he shone the light in the direction of the headstone.

He immediately recognized the boy standing

next to it. Brayden the Great was blinking in the bright light of Ethan's phone, looking *not* so very great.

"Brayden! What are you *doing* here?" said Ethan.

"I was just . . . h-hunting for Pokémon," Brayden said. "But I didn't know we were going to get l-locked in here. So now I'm kind of freaking out, actually." He wiped his runny nose with the back of his hand.

Ethan stood up, brushing off his shorts. "So you go and hide behind a headstone?" he said. "And jump out and scare me? Seriously?"

Brayden shrugged. "I wasn't *trying* to scare you."

"Did you come to help us look for Max or something?" asked Devin. "We saw him, but he ran away."

"Oh, that's, um . . . too bad," said Brayden.

"Well, we've got worse problems than that," said Carlo. "We're locked in a cemetery at night. So now we have to do the unthinkable."

Ethan was about to ask what that meant, but Brayden beat him to it. "What do you mean? Do we have to stay locked in here all night?" He sounded like he was going to cry.

Carlo pulled out his phone. "Nope, we have

to do something way worse. We have to call our parents."

Carlo tried his mom, but she was still at work. But Brayden's sister, Bella, was home. And when Ethan heard that Bella knew the groundskeeper's son and was going to help them get out of the cemetery, he nearly jumped for joy.

"That means we don't have to call Mom and Dad," he said to Devin. And for the first time in about an hour, she smiled.

When Bella rode up in a Jeep with a tall teenage boy, Ethan suddenly felt shy. He was used to thinking of her as the enemy. She was the Team Valor Gym Leader at Ivan's Ice Cream, after all.

*But tonight, she's saving our butts*, he realized. So he was going to have to rethink this whole enemy thing.

As the teenage boy approached the gate with a ring of jingling keys, Bella gave Brayden a stern look through the bars. "What're you doing here?" she said. "You were supposed to be home, watching your puppy."

Brayden shrugged. He didn't look like he was going to give up any information to his big sister.

So Bella turned to Ethan. "How about you guys?" she said. "Do you make a habit out of running around cemeteries at night?" She talked tough, but her eyes were smiling.

"We were looking for a cat," Gianna explained. "A black one. We saw it here, but it slipped away."

"Really?" said Bella, her eyebrows raised. "Brayden and I know the black cat that lives here. He's a mean, nasty stray. If I were you, I'd steer clear of him. He bit Brayden's hand last year. You should show them the scar, Brayden."

"Wait, what?" said Ethan. He suddenly wasn't feeling so shy anymore. "Brayden, you said you thought that cat was Max!"

As the iron gate swung open, Brayden was the first one through it. He didn't show off his scar. He didn't even respond to Ethan. He just started running, all the way to his bike, which was hidden in a clump of bushes.

As Ethan watched him go, the puzzle pieces started falling into place.

Brayden hadn't come to the cemetery to hunt Pokémon. *Of course he didn't,* thought Ethan. *There aren't any here!*

No, Brayden had come to spy on Team Mystic, to see if they believed his little lie about the black cat. *And to try to scare us,* Ethan realized, remembering the moaning noise he'd heard over by the tomb.

But the worst part was, he'd gotten their hopes up about Max—especially Devin's. And for that, Ethan couldn't forgive him.

He balled his hands up into fists and took off through the gate, determined to catch up with Brayden. But Carlo stepped in his path.

"Whoa, take it easy," he said. "It's not worth it—just let him go."

*Fine,* thought Ethan, his heart thudding in his ears. *I'll let him go. But then I don't ever want to see his face again. Not ever.*

# CHAPTER 11

"We should show Mrs. Applegate the photo of the cat anyway," said Devin. "Just in case it was Max!"

"It *wasn't* Max. It was a mean old stray that Brayden was trying to *trick* us into thinking was Max." Ethan wondered how many times he was going to have to tell Devin that. The girl never seemed to give up hope.

She studied the picture on her phone one more time. "I don't care what you think," she said. "I'm going to show Mrs. Applegate, just in case."

"Fine," he said. "But I'm not going with you into the library when you do."

"Fine, Krabby. Do what you want."

It was Tuesday morning, and Ethan and Devin had been fighting like six-year-olds ever since their sleepover last night at Carlo and Gianna's. Ethan knew he wasn't really mad at Devin. He was just so mad at Brayden, he didn't know what to do with himself.

*Yes, you do,* the voice in his head argued. *You need to take a break from this missing-cat thing. You need to go to Dottie's, eat a couple of doughnuts, and fight a few battles.*

So that's what he did—while Devin was across the street at the library.

At least, he went to Dottie's *planning* to battle. He sat down in his favorite booth at Dottie's and pulled out his phone. He tapped on the blue Team Mystic gym, and he prepared Raticate for battle.

"Power up, little buddy," he said, making sure the Pokémon was healthy. Then he flagged down Dottie for a doughnut. As a Trainer, he needed to power up, too.

"One Mankey, please," he said. "And a tall glass of chocolate milk."

"Coming right up!" said Dottie with a smile.

But while he was waiting for his doughnut, Ethan's phone buzzed. He spun his map to find the nearby Pokéman, and grimaced when he saw a pair of dark, flapping wings.

"Bring it on, Zubat," he muttered under his breath. "Bring. It. On."

He started firing Poké Balls at the screeching, fluttering, batlike Pokémon. He shot them off rapid fire. The Zubat squeaked and squawked and dodged every ball, but Ethan didn't let up. He fired more.

After a while, he didn't even wait until the yellow circle around the bat had shrunk. He just flung more Poké Balls, pinging them off the bat's head and slinging them into the corners of the screen.

When the app seemed to freeze up, he shook his phone. He tapped the screen, trying to get another Poké Ball.

And then he saw the message.

"No more Poké Balls."

He stared at it in disbelief.

Then he dropped his head to the table.

When Ethan felt a hand on his shoulder, he turned his face just far enough to see. It wasn't Dottie holding out the Mankey on a plate. It was Carlo.

Ethan sat straight up. "When did you get here?" he asked.

"Just in time to see you go nutso on Zubat," said Carlo. "Dottie was afraid to come over, so she sent me instead. Doughnut?" He grinned and held out the plate. The he slid into the booth across from Ethan.

Ethan took a bite of the Mankey, and instantly felt a giant blob of banana-cream filling fall into his lap. *Perfect.*

Carlo waited until Ethan had wiped his shorts clean. Then he asked, "So what was that all about? Did Zubat do you wrong in a past life or something?"

Ethan couldn't even smile. "I can't catch him," he said. "Just like I can't find Max. Or Mew. Or Mewtwo. Or even Meowth." He counted them off on his fingers—five fat failures.

Carlo nodded. "Well, I don't know if this will make you feel better or worse, but I don't think *anybody* has found Mew or Mewtwo. They may not even exist yet."

"What do you mean?" said Ethan. "They're in the Pokédex."

"Yeah, but I don't think they're in the real world yet," said Carlo. "Maybe soon—but not yet. So you're off the hook on those two."

Ethan sighed. "So there's only *two* cats I can't find. And a crazy bat I can't catch."

"I might be able to help you with Zubat, too," said Carlo. "Want me to show you a trick?"

He reached for Ethan's phone and flipped it

over, and there was Zubat—fluttering around, waiting for round two.

Ethan grimaced. "Ugh. Why is he still there?"

"Because he wants you to try to capture him, of course. What else does a Zubat have to live for?"

"Can't I just hit the run button?" Ethan whined.

"You could," said Carlo. "But Zubat aren't really that tough, once you get the hang of them. I think you should just face 'em head-on."

Carlo held the phone toward the window to collect a few Poké Balls from the PokéStop out front. Then he hit Ethan's items list and grabbed a Razz Berry.

"Okay, back to you," he said, handing Ethan the phone. "Tap on the Razz Berry to feed it to Zubat."

Ethan did, even though he didn't want to. When little hearts popped up around Zubat, he almost gagged.

"Now, this is the most important part," said Carlo. "Instead of aiming for the center of the yellow circle the way you usually do, aim for the top of it. Sometimes you just need to come at Zubat from a different angle."

Carlo made it sound so simple, but Ethan was pretty sure it wasn't. He flung the Poké Ball, and it sailed right over Zubat's head.

"Not bad," said Carlo. "Try again, a little

lower."

So Ethan did. When the ball pinged against Zubat's forehead and swallowed him up, Ethan just about fell out of the booth.

"I did it!" he said.

"Awesome!" said Carlo. "And that Razz Berry will help him stay caught, too."

Ethan held his breath while the ball wiggled. But it didn't open back up. Instead, a puff of stars floated up around the Poké Ball.

"You caught your first Zubat," said Carlo, giving Ethan a high-five. "Now you should give that annoying pest a nickname. Make it something good."

Ethan stared out the window, thinking of the most annoying name he could come up with.

*Brayden.*

He smiled and tapped the pencil next to the Zubat.

When Carlo saw what Ethan was entering, he chuckled. "Brayden's not so tough, either," he said. "You just have to figure out a way to deal with him, like you did with Zubat today."

Ethan nodded. *Carlo's a pretty smart guy,* he thought. *Brayden, on the other hand? He's just an annoying little Zubat.*

# CHAPTER 12

**B**y the time Devin showed up, Ethan was grinning from ear to ear. Maybe it was capturing Brayden the Zubat. Or maybe it was the sugar rush from his second Mankey.

"What took you so long?" he asked.

She blew the hair out of her face. "I was helping Mrs. Applegate with a project. I figure if we can't find her cat, maybe there are other ways we can help her out at the library."

"Really?" said Ethan. He didn't like the way she used the word *we* in that sentence. He was curious about this "project," but if he asked too many questions, he might get roped into helping out, too. "So what did Mrs. Applegate say about the cat in your photo?" he asked instead.

"You were right. It wasn't Max—not even close. So I need a doughnut with sprinkles, and I need it fast." Her eyes scanned the shop for Dottie.

"The Mankey was pretty good," said Ethan. "At least, the part that made it into my mouth instead of my lap. Hey, have we caught any Mankey yet?"

"I don't think so," said Devin. "Where would we even find them here in Newville? In Pheasant Ranch? I think monkeys live in trees." She waved her hand to flag down Dottie.

"Maybe," he said. Then he had another thought. "How about in playgrounds? Maybe Mankey live in parks and playgrounds—places that have monkey bars."

"You mean Mankey bars?" Devin joked.

Ethan just shook his head. Sometimes Devin's jokes were as bad as Dad's.

"What do you think?" he said. "Do you want to take a break from cat hunting today and hit a couple of parks with me to look for Mankey?"

"Sure. Why not?" When Dottie came over, Devin asked if she could please order a doughnut with sprinkles for the road.

"Sounds serious," said Dottie, sliding her pencil behind her ear. "One sprinkled doughnut, one paper bag. Coming right up." She winked and took Ethan's empty plate.

Ten minutes later, they were biking toward the park. As Ethan rode behind Devin, he saw purple sprinkles bouncing off her tires. She was leaving a little trail of them.

"If you were a lost cat, you'd be easy to track," he joked.

But she was too into her doughnut to even hear him.

Ethan made sure they stopped at every PokéStop between the doughnut shop and the park. But by the time they rode through the park gates and pulled into the bike rack, he'd only collected nine Poké Balls.

He quickly popped an egg into an incubator, just for backup. If he couldn't *catch* a lot of Pokémon today, maybe he could hatch some.

Then he showed Devin how low he was on Poké Balls. "I wish I could borrow some from you," he said. He knew Devin was a good saver. She always had a good supply of Poké Balls, not to mention a full piggy bank on her desk in her bedroom.

"Can you buy some with your Defender bonus?" she asked.

"Nah," he confessed. "I already blew that on more incense and a Lucky Egg. What if I run into a Meowth today and don't have enough ammunition to catch him?"

"Maybe you could beam him in the head with your Lucky Egg," she joked. Then she glanced over her shoulder and added, "Anyway, I'm pretty sure you're going to run into something else first."

Ethan heard the low buzzing noise, too, growing louder and closer. Brayden was coming on his stupid scooter. "Hide!" said Ethan. "Quick!"

Devin looked around. "Where? Behind the curly slide?"

"Good idea," said Ethan. Then he realized she was kidding. While he dove for cover, Devin stood perfectly still, facing Brayden head-on.

"What are you doing here?" asked Brayden as he buzzed to a stop on the sidewalk.

"What's it to you?" asked Devin.

*Ooh,* thought Ethan. *She's in sassy mode. Good!*

"Are you still mad about that cat thing?" asked Brayden. "Is that why your brother is hiding behind the curly slide?"

*Oof. Busted.*

Still, Ethan stayed hidden, pretending to search the grass for Weedle and Caterpie. He wished he could press the run button and make Brayden go away. *But he wouldn't go away. He'd just hang around like an annoying Zubat, waiting for me to come back.*

Brayden finally did leave, but it took forever. Ethan's legs were sore from squatting when Devin came over to get him out of hiding.

"He sure wants to hang out with you," she said.

"What do you mean?" he asked, wiping the grass off his knees. "He wants to *annoy* me, that's all."

She shook her head. "I think he wants to hang out with you. You used to be friends, remember?"

*That seems like a long time ago,* thought Ethan. And he didn't really want to talk about Brayden right now. "C'mon," he said. "Let's go check out the Mankey bars."

The search for Mankey at the park turned up nothing, but it was fun to be out with Devin and *not* thinking about cats. Ethan lifted his face to the breeze as they pedaled down the street. "Do you want to hit the school playground next?" he asked.

"Sure," said Devin. "Race you there!"

"You're on!"

Ethan had to admit it—Devin was pretty fast for an eight-year-old. He had to pedal his hardest and ignore every PokéStop they passed to beat her. There wasn't time to stop, and like Mom sometimes said, "Don't Pokémon GO while you pedal."

Ethan tried not to think about all the Poké Balls and Razz Berries he was missing out on!

He pulled into the school playground just seconds before Devin, and then flopped down on the grass, laughing. "That was some serious exercise. Mom would be proud of us."

"Yeah," said Devin, breathing hard. "But there's a slight problem."

"What?" Ethan sat up.

Then he heard the buzzing sound. "Oh, man. He *followed* us here?"

Devin nodded. "We flew by him really fast a couple of blocks ago. He must think we're hot on the trail of a rare Pokémon."

*Figures,* thought Ethan. *Old Brayden the Zubat can't stand being left out of anything. He just follows us around, yapping and flapping his wings.*

"So, what are you going to hide behind this time?" asked Devin. "The water fountain?"

Ethan knew she was kidding. But he also knew it was time to stop hiding.

*You could run,* Carlo had said about the Zubats. *But I think you should just face 'em head-on.*

So Ethan stood up and walked to the curb just as Brayden pulled up.

"What are you guys hunting for?" Brayden came right out and asked.

"Mankey," said Ethan. "We're hunting for Mankey." He decided to try honesty this time. After all, they hadn't found any yet. And even if they did, maybe Brayden would just capture one and then be on his way.

"Here? I don't believe you," said Brayden. "Monkeys live in trees, not in school playgrounds. I'll bet you're looking for Meowth like you were in the cemetery. Did you see him somewhere?" He looked toward Devin as if she were going to pull Meowth up on her phone and tell him exactly where to find the Pokémon.

"*Cats* live in trees too, Einstein," Ethan shot back. "So why don't you go find some. Why don't you just get lost."

His words came out sounding harsh. *But Brayden deserves it. Doesn't he?* thought Ethan.

Brayden shrugged. "Whatever." He turned his scooter around and performed a fancy little burnout.

*He's probably been practicing that move for days,* thought Ethan with a smirk. *Just waiting to show it off.*

But Brayden's next move wasn't so impressive. He hit a patch of gravel, slid sideways, and flew right off his scooter.

He squealed as he flew through the air.

Then he hit the ground with a *thud*.

# CHAPTER 13

**E**than ran toward Brayden, who was lying perfectly still.

"Is he okay?" called Devin from the sidewalk. She covered her eyes, as if she was afraid to look.

"He's fine," said Ethan. *At least I hope he's fine.*

Brayden blinked and stared up at Ethan from the ground. "Am I bleeding?"

Ethan saw the bloody knee and a trickle of blood coming from Brayden's elbow. "Not really," he fibbed. "Does anything hurt? Can you get up?" He helped Brayden slowly stand and limp out of the road.

Then Brayden caught sight of his scooter, which had skidded to the opposite curb. It looked worse off than he did. It had a long scratch on the side, but at least the wheels were still spinning.

That's when Brayden started to cry.

*Oh, man,* thought Ethan. *Here we go.*

"My p-parents spent a lot of money on that!" said Brayden. He started to walk toward the scooter, but Ethan made him sit on the curb instead.

"I'm sure it's fine," said Ethan. "I'll get it." He pulled the scooter upright, shut it off, and wheeled it toward Brayden.

"Do you want us to walk you home?" Devin asked sweetly. "Maybe we'll spot a Meowth along the way."

Ethan wished she'd consulted him first on that one, but she had a soft spot for anything that was sad or injured. And Brayden looked pretty darn sad right now.

So they walked their bikes while Brayden limped along the sidewalk, pushing his scratched scooter. He sniffled and said, "Cats don't live in trees, you know. They live in houses."

"What?"

"You said back at the playground that cats live in trees."

Ethan shot a glance at Devin. *Can you believe*

*this kid?* he wanted to say. *Even all beat up like this, he still has to be right about everything.*

But Devin didn't seem irritated. She just let him have his way. "You're right. Cats live in houses."

*Most cats, anyway,* Ethan almost said. But he'd just been struck by an idea, as sudden and powerful as Jolteon's Thunder Shock in the middle of battle.

"Cats live in houses," he repeated.

"Right," said Devin. "That's what we just said."

"So isn't that Mrs. Applegate's house over there?" He pointed toward a baby-blue house with a large wraparound porch.

"Yeah," said Devin. "But she's at the library right now, remember?"

Ethan started jogging toward the porch.

"Wait up!" he heard Devin call. "What are you doing?"

He stopped just long enough to explain. "We looked for Max near the library. We looked in the nature preserve, because of all the trees. We even looked in the cemetery!" He shot Brayden a look after that one—he couldn't help himself.

"But cats don't live in trees. They live in houses! So why didn't we ever look around Mrs. Applegate's *house?*"

He left Devin with that question as he turned

around and hurried toward the house. As he reached the wraparound porch, he slowed down.

"If I were a cat, where would I be?" he said under his breath.

First, he looked up. But Mrs. Applegate didn't have any trees around her property. *Good thing,* thought Ethan. *I'm not much of a climber.*

Then he thought of that stray cat at the cemetery, the one he'd found hiding under the cement bench—the very bench Ethan had been sitting on. So he started looking *under* things.

He looked under the hose that was rolled up on a rack near the house.

He looked under the overturned rain barrel.

He looked under a tarp that covered a small stack of wood.

By now, Devin and Brayden had joined him in Mrs. Applegate's yard.

"How about under the porch?" asked Devin. "Remember when we had a chipmunk living under ours?"

Ethan nodded. He took a step toward the porch, and then he heard the tiniest little *mew.*

Devin raised her eyebrows. She'd heard it, too. She pointed quietly to a large gap under the porch.

It was dark, full of cobwebs, and not very

inviting. And Devin showed no signs of wanting to look inside.

So Ethan laid flat on his stomach, hoping the ground wasn't wet. Then he gazed into the darkness.

It took a moment for his eyes to adjust. Then he began to make out the cracks of light and uneven textures of dirt and rocks. As he squinted to see farther beneath the porch, he suddenly realized that something was staring back at him.

Two eyes slowly blinked.

And then that something released another pitiful *mew.*

"He's here!" Ethan whispered. "Max is here."

"Can you reach him?" asked Devin.

"No way. Not even close," said Ethan.

Finding Max was one thing. Getting him out was going to be another.

Then he remembered the night at the cemetery, when Gianna had lured the stray cat toward the cage with a can of tuna.

"We need Gianna and her tuna," he said. "I'll bet Max is starving."

"And Carlo with his cage," added Devin. "Should I go try to find them?"

"Good idea," said Ethan. "Hurry!"

Devin raced toward her bike, which left

Brayden standing in the yard, looking left out and helpless.

"What can I do?" he asked.

Ethan almost told him to stay out of it—that everything was under control.

But lying here on his stomach on the ground, he saw things from a whole new angle. Everything *wasn't* under control. Max could fly out from under the porch at any moment. Devin could come back and say that Gianna and Carlo were nowhere to be found.

So Ethan could keep flinging Poké Balls at Brayden, trying to make him go away, or he could offer him a Razz Berry—and take him up on his offer to help.

"Could you go get Mrs. Applegate?" he said. "Your scooter is faster than my bike. Do you think you can ride it right now—I mean, with your injuries?"

Brayden puffed his chest out a little. "I'm on it." He wasn't limping at all anymore as he ran across the grass toward his scooter.

And then Ethan was alone. Alone in Mrs. Applegate's yard with a very scared, hungry cat.

# CHAPTER 14

Devin got back first. She dropped her bike and jogged quietly across the grass.

As she lowered herself onto her stomach beside Ethan, he raised his finger to his lips. "Careful," he whispered. "Don't scare Max away."

The cat was still staring at him with large, unblinking eyes. He hadn't moved at all.

"Oh, I hope he's okay," said Devin.

"Me, too," said Ethan. "When are Gianna and Carlo going to get here?"

"Gianna's right behind me," said Devin. "But Carlo is working. So Gianna is bringing the tuna—and the cage."

Sure enough, Gianna rode up a few seconds later on her brother's bike, the cage strapped to the back.

"Carlo isn't coming?" asked Ethan, fighting a mini panic attack. "Who's going to set up the cage?"

Devin shrugged. "We'll figure it out. We got this far, right?"

Gianna tiptoed over, holding the cage steady so that it didn't creak or jangle. She set it down on the grass and then slid off her backpack, reaching into the front pocket for the can of tuna.

"Should I open it now?" she asked.

Ethan nodded, keeping his eyes trained on Max. When Gianna pulled back the tab on the can, he saw the cat's eyes flick toward the sound. Those eyes grew wide—wide and hungry.

"It's working!" Ethan whispered. "Put it in the cage."

"Here," said Devin. "I'll move over."

As she rolled to the side, Gianna set the cage down beside Ethan. "I think you should move back a little, too," she said. "Max doesn't know you."

"Right." But as Ethan slowly slid backward, he saw Max flinch. *Is he going to run?* thought Ethan, bracing himself.

The cat didn't run. He kept his eyes fixed on

Ethan and his nose on that can of tuna.

"Oh, I wish Mrs. Applegate would come!" said Gianna. "Do you think Brayden is getting her?"

"I hope so," said Ethan. But he didn't take his eyes off Max. The cat was slowly creeping forward, sniffing the air. Paw by paw, he inched toward the cage.

As Max took his first step into the cage, Ethan could barely breathe. After two more steps, Max reached the tuna. Then, with one last wary glance at Ethan, he sat down and started to eat.

As he gobbled up that delicious meal, Ethan oh so slowly reached for the door on the front of the cage and slid it closed. *Click!*

"We did it!" Devin and Gianna started jumping up and down. Ethan would have celebrated, too, but he didn't want to scare Max, who wasn't all that happy about suddenly being locked in.

That's when they heard the buzz of the scooter. Devin ran to the street to greet Brayden and Mrs. Applegate, who was flying after him on her bike. She was riding so fast that her hair had come loose from its bun, but her eyes were bright.

"Max?" she called.

"We found him!" said Devin. "He's safe. Max is home, safe and sound."

As Mrs. Applegate raced toward her precious

kitty, Brayden hobbled toward Ethan. A trickle of blood was drying on his leg from his scooter wipe-out, but he had a grin on his face.

"You did it?" he asked. "You caught him?"

"*We* caught him," said Ethan. "You're the one who gave me the idea to look here at the house." Then he did something he thought he'd never do in a million years.

He gave Brayden a high-five.

That night at dinner, Ethan could hardly wait for Mom to ask the question.

She said grace. She asked Dad how work went at the bank today. And she seemed excited to hear that Max had been found. Then she told Devin to please drink her milk and asked Ethan to at least *try* the spinach.

Finally, Ethan couldn't take it anymore. "Mom!" he said in exasperation. "Ask me what I learned from Pokémon GO today. Go ahead, ask me."

Mom laughed. "Okay, dear son, tell me what you learned from Pokémon GO today."

He cleared his throat, like Dad usually did before saying something important. "I learned that sometimes you have to come at things from a new angle."

"You mean like when you're lying on your stomach under a porch?" asked Devin.

"Yeah, something like that," said Ethan, laughing. "But when you're dealing with annoying pests, too. Like Zubat."

"And Brayden?" asked Devin.

"Right. I mean, he's always going to be annoying. But sometimes, you just have to toss him a Razz Berry."

"Huh?"

Even Devin looked confused by that one, so Ethan tried again. "Sometimes you just have to include him in things."

"Ah, right," said Dad. "Good one."

Mom seemed impressed by that answer, too, so Ethan figured he was pretty much good on the "What did you learn from Pokémon GO?" question for the next few nights now.

"How about you, Devin?" asked Mom. "What did you learn from Pokémon GO today?"

Devin scrunched up her nose. She was in the hot seat now. "I learned that . . . um . . . cats live in houses?"

Mom cocked her head. "Hmm . . . maybe you'll have something better tomorrow."

# CHAPTER 15

On the way to Dottie's Doughnuts in the morning, Ethan heard his phone buzz.

"Devin, pull over for a sec," he hollered to his sister. After Brayden's major scooter wipe-out, Ethan had been especially careful never to check his phone while he was on something with wheels.

He pulled to the curb and slid his phone out of his pocket.

There, on the screen, was a Pokémon egg. "Oh?" said Ethan, reading the word above the egg. "It's hatching!"

He loved the part where the egg started to crack

and something completely unexpected popped out.

Devin did, too. She wheeled her bike over to watch.

But they were both blown away by what came out of that egg.

"Meowth!" shouted Ethan. "Yes, yes, yes! I can't believe it! We've been looking for him for *days* now. And then the cool cat just cracks out of an egg when he's good and ready."

"That's the thing about cats," said Devin, shaking her head. "Sometimes you have to wait and let them come to you. Hey, speaking of hard-to-find cats, can we stop at the library and say hi to Max?"

"Sure," said Ethan. "Do you think he'll remember us from yesterday?"

Devin shrugged. "Maybe we should have brought another can of tuna."

When they reached the library, Ethan glanced across the street at Dottie's Doughnuts. "Can we grab a doughnut first?" he asked Devin. "I'm seriously craving a Mankey and a big glass of milk."

"No," she said right away. "Let's go to the library first."

"But, wait, I think I see Gianna's and Carlo's bikes in Dottie's rack. Let's go get them."

"Ethan, just come on!" said Devin, waving him

toward the library door.

"Okay, okay. Why are you being so weird?"

Ethan parked his bike and followed his sister into the dark, cool building.

Mrs. Applegate was at the front desk, looking very well rested. And there was Max, curled up on a pile of books as if he'd never been gone.

"Kids!" said the librarian, jumping up. "I've been waiting for you."

"You have?" asked Ethan.

"Yes. Follow me."

He turned toward Devin, who didn't seem at all surprised by Mrs. Applegate's mysterious behavior. "What's going on?" he asked Devin.

She laughed and pretended to zip her lips. She had a secret, and she wasn't telling.

Mrs. Applegate led them down the hall toward the activity room. The hallway seemed a lot brighter than Ethan remembered it being. Had Mrs. Applegate painted? Or was it just her good mood reflecting off the walls?

When she reached the door at the end of the hall, she stopped. "This," she announced, "is the new Poké GO Room."

"You mean Poké*mon* GO," Devin corrected her.

"Oh, yes," said Mrs. Applegate with a smile.

"I'm still learning."

She opened the door and let Ethan step in first.

When he did, the room erupted with noise. "Surprise!"

Carlo and Gianna were already there, jumping up from a circular table that had been painted half red, half white—like a Poké Ball!

Ethan spun in a circle to take it all in. He saw framed pictures of Pokémon on the wall. They were Devin's photos! There was a Jigglypuff by a coffee cup, a Beedrill sitting on a bike seat, and a fox-crossing poster made from her picture of Vulpix.

When Devin saw Ethan looking at the photos, she blushed.

"So, wait," said Ethan. "Was this the mysterious project you were helping Mrs. Applegate with yesterday?"

Devin nodded, smiling from ear to ear.

"And you guys were in on this?" he asked Gianna and Carlo.

Carlo shrugged. "I helped make the table with some paint from the hardware store."

"I was pretty much just moral support," said Gianna. "We figured you could use a pick-me-up after getting locked in the cemetery with your buddy Brayden."

"And that whole going-crazy-on-a-helpless-Zubat incident at the doughnut shop," Carlo added with a grin.

"Wow." Ethan sat at the Poké Ball table and ran his hand over the smooth paint. "So we can really play here?" he asked Mrs. Applegate.

She nodded. "You kids put so much time into looking for Max. I wanted to do something for you in return."

As if on cue, Max sauntered into the room, flicking his tail and checking out the new digs.

"There is one rule, though," said Mrs. Applegate, holding up a finger.

*Uh-oh,* thought Ethan. *Here we go.*

"The rule is that every time you come to play, you have to check out at least one book," said Mrs. Applegate with a smile.

Ethan relaxed his shoulders. "That's not so bad," he said. "My mom will be thrilled with that rule."

Devin nodded. "For sure."

"Can we start right away?" asked Ethan. He pulled out his phone and looked at Mrs. Applegate expectantly.

She still looked a bit stern, but her eyes were smiling. "Certainly. I'll leave you kids to it." She left the room, with Max trailing close behind.

Ethan cracked his knuckles and stretched his fingers. "Okay, Spearow, old buddy, old pal. Let's see how you've been doing." He tapped on the gym, happy to see that it was still blue—ruled by Team Mystic.

"Are we still the only Defenders?" asked Carlo, plunking down beside him.

Ethan nodded. He swiped through his own avatar page, with DogBoy918 standing next to Spearow. Then he swiped to the right to see Carlo's: Carlozard14 standing next to Fearow.

"Do you want to play, Gia?" asked Devin, offering her friend her phone.

"Thanks!" said Gianna, finding a spot at the table. Then she said to her brother, "You're the only two Defenders *for now*. But as soon as I level up this gym, Giadude99 is going to have her own page, too, with a Beedrill by her side."

"I believe you," said Ethan, laughing. Gianna was already a tough fighter, especially for a player without her own phone. "But when other teams see this Pokémon GO room, the whole gym might be up for grabs. We'd better get busy earning some prestige points for Team Mystic."

He knew exactly which Pokémon he wanted to train first. "C'mere, Meowth," he said. "Let's see what you've got."

On the way out of the library, Ethan almost forgot to grab a book. But Devin reminded him.

"Should we look at the mysteries?" she asked.

Ethan groaned. "I've had enough mystery for a few days. Let's look for something else."

Devin poked through the nonfiction shelf. When she reached the P's, she slid out a book. "This one is perfect!" she said, showing him the cover. *Photography Tips and Tricks.*

"I don't know, Devin," he said. "I think you could pretty much *write* that book already."

She flashed a proud smile.

Ethan wandered down toward the other end of the aisle. "How about this one for me?" he asked, pulling a shiny book from the shelf. *"Bats and Their Habitats."*

Devin laughed. "I thought you hated bats," she said. "What happened to the I Hate Zubat fan club? I was going to make us T-shirts!"

Ethan shrugged. "I don't hate them anymore," he said. "I mean, I don't *love* them, but I'm learning to like them a little."

"Are you going to use that one at dinner tonight,

when Mom asks what you learned from Pokémon GO?"

"I don't know," said Ethan. "It's pretty early in the day. Let's go to Dottie's and see if I can think of something even better."

# Do you Love pLaying Pokémon GO?

Check out these books for fans of Pokémon GO!

Catching the
Jigglypuff Thief
ALEX POLAN

Following Meowth's
Footprints
ALEX POLAN

# Coming Soon!

Chasing Butterfree
ALEX POLAN

Cracking the
Magikarp Code
ALEX POLAN

Available wherever books are sold!